Dolphinella

Dolphinella

By Kit Wright   Illustrated by Peter Bailey

For Eleanor B
K.W.

For Thomos Paul
P.B.

Scholastic Children's Books,
Commonwealth House, 1-19 New Oxford Street,
London WC1A 1NU, UK
a division of Scholastic Ltd

London ~ New York ~ Toronto ~ Sydney ~ Auckland
Mexico City ~ New Delhi ~ Hong Kong

First published in hardback by Scholastic Ltd, 1995
This paperback edition published by Scholastic Ltd, 2000

Text copyright © Kit Wright, 1995
Illustrations copyright © Peter Bailey, 1995

ISBN 0 590 13355 1

Printed in Belgium

Ella went for a picnic
Down by the riverside
Where the waters roll
On the foaming stones
And the small white flowers hide.

Nobody told a secret
That Ella wanted to keep:
Ella was bored and Ella was tired
So Ella . . .
Fell asleep!

When altogether a different thing
Ella began to be . . .

Began to be
A grey shape nosing
On through the climbing waves,
Where the great grey ocean makes its house
Of mountains and of caves.

For Ella grew in the breakers
Rubbery, silk and strong,
And her feet became a whacking tail
And her arms were flippers
To flap and flail

As smoothly she raced along . . .

DOLPHINELLA she was!
With a gang of dolphins round her
Leaping her back and brushing her fin,
So very happy they'd found her!

They swam along by a power-boat
And the people leaned over the side
And laughed as Dolphinella walked
On her tail . . . or she hitched a ride
On the churning waves at the bow that made her
Swoop and surf and glide!

Then Dolphinella went diving down on her own,

Down to the deep dark
Ocean floor
Where strange eyes watched
From the drapes of weed,

And there on his throne sat Neptune,
King of the Sea!
The one that all of the ocean feared
With his jewelled crown and his streaming beard
And his wild green eyes as ANGRY
As they could be!

"Oh, I am the one to find that boot
And bear it home to your deep-sea cellar:
Leave it to me!"
Said Dolphinella.

She flapped her flippers
And whacked her tail
And sped off on
The sea-boot trail . . .

While mighty Neptune, King of the deep blue sea,
Sat there scratching his head.
"There was a dolphin here, it seemed to me,
And what was that
She said?"

Meanwhile Dolphinella nosed
Round the bones of a wreck
Where skeletons lay . . .
And she peered under stones
And she looked in the weed:

There were crawly creatures,
Yes, indeed,
But there wasn't a boot,
No way!

Until . . .

She slipped round a big green rock
And spied . . .
THE BOOT
With a CONGER EEL inside!

"Sorry, Conger,
That home's not yours,"
She said, and she flipped him
Out of doors!

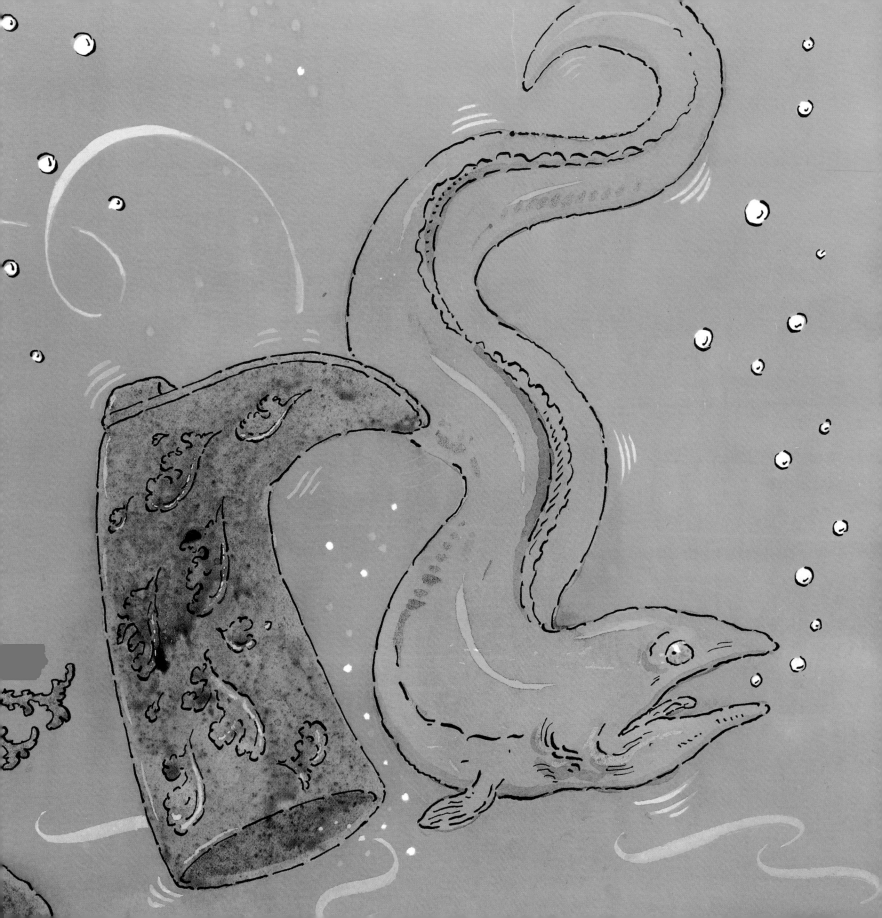

Back with the boot to Neptune's cave
She went. "Oh, thank you!" Neptune cried.
"Now I'll give *you* a precious gift
To bear home on the foaming tide!"

And out of his crown he plucked a shining jewel
And tucked it under
Her flipper to keep.

"Thank you, Neptune!" said Dolphinella
And swam off up
From the dark of the deep . . .

And her dolphin friends said, "Nice to see you again!"
And the folks in the boat all yelled,
"She's back! Yippee!"

And Ella woke on the riverbank.
Her mother said "Ella,
You were sleeping, dear!
Where did you get that bright blue pebble?
It's a lovely one!
Did you find it here?

My, you're a clever old
Sleepyhead!"

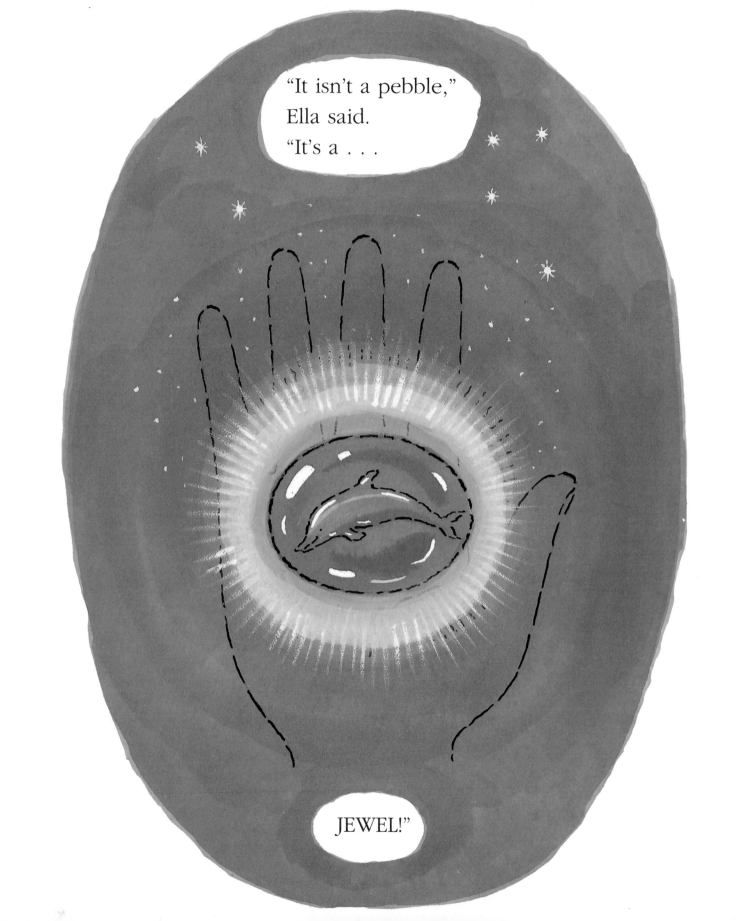